You do not need to read this page –
just get on with the book!

First published in 2001 in Great Britain by
Barrington Stoke Ltd
18 Walker Street, Edinburgh, EH3 7LP
www.barringtonstoke.co.uk

This edition first published in 2009

This edition based on Problems with a Python, published by
Barrington Stoke in 1999

ISBN: 978-1-84299-793-2

Printed in Great Britain by Bell & Bain Ltd

Meet The Author - Jeremy Strong

What is your favourite animal?
A cat
What is your favourite boy's name?
Magnus Pinchbottom
What is your favourite girl's name?
Wobbly Wendy
What is your favourite food?
Chicken Kiev (I love garlic)
What is your favourite music?
Soft
What is your favourite hobby?
Sleeping

Meet The Illustrator - Scoular Anderson

What is your favourite animal?
Humorous dogs
What is your favourite boy's name?
Orlando
What is your favourite girl's name?
Esmerelda
What is your favourite food?
Garlicky, tomatoey pasta
What is your favourite music?
Big orchestras
What is your favourite hobby?
Long walks

This is for everyone
who suffers from
an older sister ... or brother

Contents

1 A Visitor   1

2 Shock! Horror!   9

3 Flies, Bees and False Teeth   19

4 A Monkey in the Hall   27

5 A Strange Boy   37

6 The Snake Appears at Last   47

7 What Happened in the End?   55

Chapter 1
A Snake Comes to Stay

Adam pressed his nose up to the glass tank.

"It's not a very big snake," he told his friend, Gary.

Gary rolled his eyes. "I'm telling you, she's over a metre long."

"I thought pythons were *huge*."

"Not when they're small," Gary said.
"This one is still a baby."

Adam tapped the glass, but the snake
didn't move. "What do you feed it on?"

"She's not an 'it' and you won't need to
feed her," Gary told him. "We're only going
away for a week to stay with my gran.

She won't need a meal for days. She ate a rat for supper last night."

"Urrgh!" said Adam.

"What did you think pythons ate? Ice cream?"

Gary took the lid off the tank. He pulled out the python. She lay across his arms.

"She's all slimy," Adam said.

"Don't be stupid. Snakes only *look* slimy. It's because their skin shines."

"Yeah?" said Adam.

"Yeah. Go on. You hold her."

Gary dumped the python into Adam's arms. Adam almost dropped her. He stood there, while the snake wound itself around his left arm.

"She likes you to stroke her," Gary said. "You will look after her while I'm away, won't you? You don't even have to get her out of the tank if you don't want to ... I mean, if you're *scared* ..."

Adam felt the python's hard, flat head push up under his chin. Then her head slid up Adam's cheek. Her tongue began to flicker. Adam gulped.

"I'm not scared," he said.

"That's all right then," smiled Gary. "I can see she likes you. She sticks her tongue in my ear too. If she tries to nibble your neck just keep very still."

"What!"

"Just a joke," Gary said. "Thanks for looking after her. I'll see you in a week."

"Yeah, OK. Bye."

A few moments later, the front door banged and Gary had gone. Adam was alone with a python.

This snake was no fun as a pet. She just lay there in the tank. There must be something Adam could do with the python. But what?

Chapter 2
Shock! Horror!

"How much longer are you going to be?"

Adam's big sister Emma banged on the bathroom door. It was Sunday, and Emma was Getting-Ready-For-The-Boyfriend.

She stood outside the door with her arms full of shampoo and soap and bath foam. She had her lipstick and eye make-up with her too.

"Just hurry up, will you? You've been in there hours and hours. Rob will be here very soon."

"I'm on the loo," said Adam. "You can't hurry that sort of thing."

Emma stomped back to her room. Adam smiled to himself. He was not sitting on the loo. He was standing in the bath and draping the python round the shower head.

This is going to be fun!

Adam got out of the bath. He pulled the shower screen across so that the snake was hidden. From down below he heard the *bing-bong* of the doorbell. Emma was back in a flash, banging on the door.

"Let me in!" she yelled. "Rob's here! You've made me late. I haven't even washed my hair or anything!"

Adam flushed the loo and opened the door.

"It's all yours," he said.

Emma pushed past him. She was very angry.

"I'm going to kill you!" she hissed.

"Oh no, not again," Adam said with a smile.

"Ha, ha," said Emma.

She slammed the door and locked it. Adam went to his room and sat on his bed. He began to count.

"One, two, three, four, five, six ..."

"Aaaaargh! Eeek! Oh my God! Aaargh!"

The bathroom door shook as Emma tried to open it in a hurry. The lock shot back. The door was flung open and out rushed Emma with just a towel round her.

"Snake!" she yelled. "Snake in the shower!"

Emma ran down the stairs and into the sitting room. Her amazed parents just looked at her. An even more amazed boyfriend looked at her too.

"Wow," muttered Rob, his eyes popping. "Nice dress."

"There's a snake in the shower!" yelled Emma. "Aren't you going to save me?"

Adam's parents looked from Emma to Rob and back to Emma. They were waiting to see what would happen next. Rob started to move towards the sitting room door. His spotty face had gone red. He nodded. He was thinking.

"You did say a snake?" he asked.

"It was hissing at me from the shower head," Emma told him. "Go on, go and catch it."

"Er, I'm not very good with snakes," said Rob.

Emma folded her arms and glared at her boyfriend.

"You're scared," she snapped.

"No, no," said Rob. "It's just that when I try to catch them they sort of slip out of my hands – I can't get a grip."

Adam's dad hid a smile and went to the stairs.

"Go and get dressed Emma. It's only Gary's python. Adam's looking after it while Gary's with his gran. Didn't you know?"

"Nobody tells me *anything*."

Adam's mum put an arm round Emma.

"I expect Adam let her out by mistake. We did tell him to make sure she stayed in the tank."

"I'll kill him," muttered Emma.

Rob smiled at Emma. "I think you look nice in that towel," he said.

"Oh, shut up!" snapped Emma.

"Right," said Rob, and he stared at the floor.

No-one said a word.

Adam's dad called down from the bathroom.

"All clear! The snake's back in the tank." He stood at the top of the stairs. "Adam says the snake must have got out somehow."

Emma went back into the bathroom and shut the door.

Inside his bedroom Adam stuck his head under his pillow. What a laugh! So, what could he do next?

Chapter 3
Flies, Bees and False Teeth

Monday came and Adam had to go to school. Sunday had been such fun that Adam planned to take the python with him. He stuffed the sleeping snake into his school bag.

Adam's friends would think it was great when he turned up with a python. His teacher, Mrs Batty, was always telling them

to bring in things that the others might like to see. Last week, Linda had taken in a piece of amber with a dead fly stuck inside it. Adam's friend Gary told her that he had a bar of soap at home with a moth stuck on it. He could bring that in. Linda told Gary he was stupid. Gary told Linda that she was more stupid than he was.

Adam thought Gary was right. Linda was a stupid bore. She was very pretty, but she could be mean. She could sting like a bee.

Now that Adam had his python he could give Linda the shock of her life.

When Adam got to school there was a drama going on. Some of the boys had been playing football. The ball had hit Mrs Batty hard on the back of her head. Her false teeth had shot out of her mouth. Half the class were hunting for them. Adam put his bag in the classroom and went off to help look.

"I never knew Mrs Batty had false teeth," he said.

"You don't know anything, full stop," Linda told him.

Adam frowned and said nothing. After all, he had a dark secret in the bottom of his school bag.

At last, Mrs Batty's teeth were found in an apple tree. Everyone went into school. Adam grabbed his bag and sat down next to Martin.

"What do you think I've got in here?" he said.

"I don't know. What?"

"A snake. It's Gary's. I'm looking after her for him."

Martin's eyes grew big. "You haven't got Gary's python in there?"

"Yeah. Look."

Adam put his hand into his bag and felt down to the very bottom. The only thing down there that felt at all like a snake was a football sock. Adam took his hand out of the bag. His face was white.

"Oh dear," he groaned. "She's got out."

The news was soon all round the class. Mrs Batty looked at everyone. She could tell something was going on, but what? She knew that if she said nothing they would soon give their secret away.

Half the class thought Adam *had* got a snake somewhere. They were on his side. Linda and her friends were on the other side.

"You did *not* bring a python to school," she hissed. She turned to her friends. "He's just trying to make himself look big."

"No, I'm not!" Adam's face was a deep red.

"Look at his ears! They're on fire! That's how I know he's lying," she told everyone and she went off with her friends.

"Where is the snake now?" one of
Adam's friends asked.

Chapter 4
A Monkey in the Hall

Mrs Batty lined up everyone in 6B at the classroom door and they went down to the hall. As they sat down with the other children, some of them began looking round. They were trying to spot the snake.

Mr Twigg, the headteacher, began to talk. What were 6B looking for? Their eyes were all over the place.

"6B! Have you got a problem?" he asked.

"No, Mr Twigg," replied 6B.

"What have I just said to you, Tracey?"

Tracey gulped. The whole school turned to look at her. Even Adam turned to look. As he did so, he saw something high up on one wall of the hall.

Adam froze.

"Um," began Tracey. "You said, 'Good morning everyone', Mr Twigg." The rest of the school laughed.

"You haven't heard a word I said, Tracey. You must do better from now on. Everyone stand. We are going to sing today's song – *All Things Bright and Beautiful*."

Adam could not take his eyes off the wall-bars at the far end of the hall. The snake was folded around the very top bar, where anyone could see her. Adam was about to tell Martin but he stopped himself. No-one must know.

As Adam sang with the others, he kept his fingers crossed. He hoped that nobody would spot the snake so high up. Maybe when the hall was empty again, he could creep back and catch the python.

Adam tried not to look at the wall-bars. But every now and then, he had to take a quick peek to see if the snake was still there. She seemed to be fast asleep.

Please, oh please stay where you are!

They seemed to be sitting there for a very long time. Then as soon as they were back in class Adam put up his hand. "I need to go to the loo," he told Mrs Batty.

"Cross your legs," she said.

"They are crossed, and I still need to go."

Mrs Batty gave a sigh. "All right, Adam, go to the toilet if you must."

Adam shot from his seat and raced from the classroom. He ran down the stairs and slipped into the hall. He looked up at the wall-bars at the far end. The snake was still there.

Adam ran across the hall and began to climb. Soon he got to the sleepy snake.

"Come on," he said. "Time to get you back into my bag. Come on."

But as Adam spoke, the hall doors were flung open. A class of six-year-olds rushed in and began racing round in their vests and pants.

Miss Raza, their teacher, walked in and began to tell them what to do. "Run round, everyone! Jump as high as you can!"

The six-year-olds jumped about like baby rabbits. They yelled at each other. The noise woke the snake.

"Don't move!" Adam hissed at the snake.

But she began to slide along the bar.

"Come back!" said Adam. "Come back, you stupid thing! Can you hear me?"

Adam went after the snake, trying not to make a sound.

Then one of the children stood still and pointed at the wall-bars. "A monkey! There's a monkey!"

Chapter 5
A Strange Boy

Everyone stopped jumping about. They all shouted. "Monkey! Monkey!"

Miss Raza ran over to the wall-bars and gazed up. "Adam – what *are* you doing?" she asked. "How long have you been up there?"

"I don't know," said Adam. He clung to the top bar.

"You don't know? Does Mrs Batty know you are up there?"

"No."

"Come down at once."

Adam crept down the bars. Miss Raza was not pleased. "What were you doing up there?"

"Um ... hiding," he told her.

How do I talk my way out of this?

"Hiding! What from?"

"A – a spider," said Adam. "I'm scared of spiders. I saw one and went up the wall-bars to escape. Then you came in and I was scared to come down again."

"You odd child," said Miss Raza, and she shook her head.

"He's a monkey," shouted one girl.

"He's a baby," said one boy. "I'm not scared of spiders. Only babies are scared of spiders."

"And elephants," added a small girl.

"Yes, and elephants."

"That's enough everyone," said Mrs Raza. "Adam, go back to your class at once. Mrs Batty will be asking where you are. I shall tell her your silly story at breaktime. Go on, off you go."

Adam went back to the classroom. At least no-one had spotted the snake. She had slipped away. But where had she gone? She could be anywhere.

Breaktime came. In the playground Adam told his friends about the python on the wall-bars. Some way off, Linda was

telling all *her* friends that it was mad to think there was a snake in the school.

Adam didn't listen to Linda. He knew the snake was in school. The problem was that he didn't know *where*, because she wasn't sleeping on the wall-bars any more.

Adam and his friends set off on a snake hunt. They went to look in the cloakrooms. But they didn't find the snake.

Where can that snake have got to?

"What do we *do* if we do see it?" Tracey asked, as they set off to look in the playground.

Tracey will run a mile
if she sees the snake

"You call to her. You say 'Sit, stay ...'
What do you think you do?" said Adam.
"Just tell me and I'll come and get her."

Mrs Batty looked out at them all from the window of the staff room. Miss Raza stood next to her.

"That Adam is very odd," Miss Raza said. "I found him at the top of the wall-bars in the hall this morning."

"Did you?" Mrs Batty replied. "That's an odd place to find a toilet. He told me he had to go."

"Odd boy," they both said at the same time, and they shook their heads.

A moment later they heard loud yells from below.

Chapter 6
The Snake Appears at Last

"Aaargh!"

The school caretaker rushed into the playground. He was waving a mop and swinging a toilet brush round and round his head.

"Snake!" yelled the caretaker. "There's a snake in my office!"

There was panic. Cries of 'Snake! Snake!' filled the air. The little ones began to cry. So did many of the older children. The caretaker waved his mop and toilet brush.

Teachers came rushing out. They tried to calm the children down.

"Are you sure it was a snake?" Mr Twigg, the headmaster, asked the caretaker.

"It was a snake," he told Mr Twigg.
"It was huge. It was a python. I saw one on
TV the other night. They can eat whole pigs
you know, and goats."

Over the din in the playground a new
sound could be heard. It was a siren.
First there were two sirens, then three,
then four, then five sirens.

The police were on their way to the
school. So were the fire engines. Adam's heart
sank.

Policemen rushed into the school. Firemen got out their hoses.

A lot of people were standing outside the school fence. They were trying to see what was going on.

"It's a fire," said an old lady.

The teachers gathered the children together at the far end of the school field. Adam found himself standing next to Linda.

"I told you there was a snake," he said.

He wanted her to know that he had been telling the truth, even if everyone was going to be very cross with him. Linda said nothing.

Inside the school, people were running about. They looked for the snake everywhere. But for a long time, she was nowhere to be found.

It was a policeman who found the snake in the end. She was under a pile of sacks, in the corner of the caretaker's office. The policeman began to laugh. He picked up the snake in both hands. He marched out to the playground and went across to the headteacher and the caretaker.

"Is this your snake?" he asked.

The caretaker stared at the thick piece of old, brown hose in the policeman's arms. It *looked* just like a python with its grubby yellow marks. But it was just a piece of old, brown hose.

The caretaker went very red. He rubbed his bald head. Mr Twigg began to laugh. The teachers began to laugh. Everyone began to laugh.

Linda turned on Adam. "I told everyone you never had a *real* snake in school," she said.

Chapter 7
What Happened in the End?

Everyone went away and the playground was empty again. The children lined up in their classes and went back into school. They were all talking to each other but nobody spoke to Adam. His friends didn't come near him. They thought he had tricked them. There had never been a snake at all.

When they got back to class, Adam found

himself sitting alone. The only person who would look at him was Linda. She gave him a mocking smile. But Adam did not see it. He was thinking of something else. Where *was* the python now?

Adam spent the afternoon thinking and

thinking. The python must have gone somewhere. Adam sat in his seat and gazed into space. Mrs Batty looked at him and shook her head.

"Are you all right, Adam?" she asked.

Adam jumped. "What?" he said.

"What's the matter with you?" said Mrs Batty. "Has the caretaker upset you?"

Adam stared back at her. She had given him an idea. That *must* be it. Adam jumped up from his chair and raced for the door.

"Where are you going?" cried Mrs Batty.

"The loo!" yelled Adam.

"Not up the wall-bars, please," Mrs Batty called after him.

Adam ran all the way to the caretaker's office. He banged on the door. There was no reply. Adam pushed open the door and looked inside.

"Hello? Anyone in?"

There was still no reply. Adam went in.

The room stank of string and socks and polish. It was a mess. There were tins and dusters and brooms. Five dirty coffee mugs stood on the table.

Adam was sure the snake was in that room somewhere and that the caretaker *had* seen her.

Adam looked under the tins and dusters.
He looked on the shelves. No python.

Adam opened a drawer. Inside, fast asleep,
was the python. He picked up the snake.
Then he ran back to the cloakroom to hide
the snake away. It was only five minutes to
hometime.

Adam went back to class feeling great. As he walked in, everyone turned to took at him.

"Better?" asked Mrs Batty.

"Brill!" said Adam with a grin. He sat down.

The bell went for hometime and the children rushed for the cloakroom. They grabbed their bags and coats.

"Some snake," Linda said to Adam.

Adam gave a shrug and set off for home. He was pleased with the way things had turned out. No-one had been cross with him. He had found the snake.

The funny thing was that even now Adam didn't have the python with him. But he knew where she was. He had put her in the bottom of Linda's bag.